Where Is Speedy?

小快在哪裡？

Jill McDougall 著

王祖民 繪

"We must clean Speedy's *tank," said Mom to Julie.

"Okay," said Julie. She took Speedy out of the tank and put him in the sink.

*為生字，請參照生字表

2

Speedy did not like the sink, but he could not get out. "It won't be for long," said Julie as she went off to clean the tank.

Dad came into the room. He wanted to wash his hands in the sink.

"Hello, Speedy," said Dad.

He took Speedy out of the sink and put him in a big *pot.

4

Speedy did not like the big pot, but he could not get out.

"It won't be for long," said Dad as he washed his hands.

*Nanna came into the room. She wanted
to cook soup in the big pot.
"Hello, Speedy," said Nanna.
She took Speedy out of the big pot
and put him in a little pot.

Speedy did not like the little pot, but he could not get out.

"It won't be for long," said Nanna as she made the soup.

*Pop came into the room. He wanted to make tea in the little pot.

"Hello, Speedy," said Pop.

He took Speedy out of the little pot and put him in a box.

Speedy did not like the box, but he could not get out.

"It won't be for long," said Pop as he made the tea.

*Uncle Jerry came into the room. He wanted to use the box for his CDs.

"Hello, Speedy," said Uncle Jerry.

He took Speedy out of the box and put him
in the trash can.

Speedy liked the trash can.

Mom came into the room. She had some *sand from Speedy's tank.

She put it in the trash can on top of Speedy. Speedy did not like the sand, but he could not get out.

The trash can was full so Mom took it outside.

Julie came into the room and looked

in the sink.

"Where is Speedy?" she said.

"In the big pot," said Dad.

"No, he isn't," said Nanna.

"I made soup in the big pot.

Speedy is in the little pot."

"No, he isn't," said Uncle Jerry.

"I put my CDs in the box.

Speedy is in the trash can."

"No, he isn't," said Pop. "I made tea

in the little pot. Speedy is in the box."

"Oh dear!" said Dad.

"The trash can went outside."

Julie ran outside. The trash can was there but she could not find Speedy anywhere.

"Speedy is *lost," she told everyone.

Mom came back into the room.

Everyone looked at her.

"WHERE IS SPEEDY?" they said.

"In his tank," said Mom.

"I found him in the trash can."

"Poor Speedy," said Julie.

"Speedy is very happy now," said Mom.

"Come and look."

They went to his tank.

Speedy was sitting on a rock.

But what was he eating?

"It's a *pea," said Mom.

"Speedy found it in the trash can."

生字表

adj.=形容詞， n.=名詞

p.2

媽媽對茱莉說:「我們得清一清小快的飼養箱。」
茱莉說:「好啊。」她把小快從飼養箱裡拿出來,放進水槽裡。

p.3

小快不喜歡那個水槽,但是他沒辦法出來。
茱莉一邊走去清理飼養箱,一邊說:「不會太久的。」

p.4

爸爸走進廚房,他想在水槽裡洗手。
爸爸說:「哈囉,小快。」
他把小快從水槽裡拿出來,放進一個大鍋子裡。

p.5

小快不喜歡那個大鍋子,但是他沒辦法出來。
爸爸邊洗著手邊說:「不會太久的。」

p.6

奶奶走進廚房，她想用大鍋子煮湯。
奶奶說：「哈囉，小快。」
她把小快從大鍋子裡拿出來，放進一個小茶壺裡。

p.7

小快不喜歡那個小茶壺，但是他沒辦法出來。
奶奶邊煮著湯邊說：「不會太久的。」

p.8

爺爺走進廚房，他想用小茶壺泡茶。
爺爺說：「哈囉，小快。」
他把小快從小茶壺裡拿出來，放進一個箱子裡。

p.9

小快不喜歡那個箱子，但是他沒辦法出來。
爺爺邊泡著茶邊說：「不會太久的。」

p.10

傑瑞叔叔走進廚房，他想用
那個箱子裝他的 CD。
傑瑞叔叔說：「哈囉，小快。」
他把小快從箱子裡拿出來，
放進垃圾桶裡。
小快喜歡那個垃圾桶。

p.12

媽媽走進廚房，手裡握著小快飼養箱裡
的一些沙子。
她把沙子倒進垃圾桶裡，剛好倒在小快
身上。
小快不喜歡那些沙子，但是他沒辦法出
來。
垃圾桶滿了，所以媽媽把它拿到外面
去。

p.14-15

茱莉跑進廚房，往水槽裡
看。
她說：「小快呢？」
爸爸說：「在大鍋子裡。」

p.16-17

奶奶說:「不，他不在那裡，我拿大鍋子來煮湯了，小快在小茶壺裡。」

爺爺說:「不，他不在那裡，我拿小茶壺來泡茶了，小快在箱子裡。」

傑瑞叔叔說:「不，他不在那裡，我拿箱子來裝我的 CD 了，小快在垃圾桶裡。」

爸爸說:「喔，天啊！垃圾桶剛剛被拿出去了。」

p.18

茱莉跑了出去。垃圾桶還在，但是就是找不到小快。

她告訴大家:「小快不見了。」

p.19

媽媽回到廚房，大家都看著她。

他們說：「小快呢？」

媽媽說：「在他的飼養箱裡啊，我在垃圾桶裡找到他的。」

茱莉說：「可憐的小快。」

p.20

媽媽說：「小快現在快樂得很呢，過來看看。」

他們走近小快的飼養箱。

小快正坐在石頭上，不過，他好像正在吃著什麼東西。

p.22

媽媽說：「那是豌豆啦，小快在垃圾桶裡找到的。」

(2) The fish is in the tank.
My pencil is not by the book.
The dog is under the table.
The dinner is in the pot.
The bug is not on the rock.
The flowers are between the trees.

句型練習

Someone Is (Somewhere)....

在「小快在哪裡?」這個故事中,我們見到了許多有關 "Speedy is (somewhere)...." (小快在 [某處]) 的用法,現在我們就一起來練習 "Someone is (somewhere)...." (某人在 [某處]) 的句型吧!

1 請跟著 CD 的 Track 4,唸出下面這些表示「位置」的英文。

by the book

in the tank

under the table

on the rock

between the trees

in the pot

2 請仔細聽 CD 的 Track 5，利用左頁的提示完成以下的句子：

Where is Speedy?

Speedy is not in the box.

Speedy is not in the trash can.

Speedy is in his tank.

The fish is _____.

My pencil is not _____.

The dog is _____.

The dinner is _____.

The bug is not _____.

The flowers are _____.

跟烏龜作朋友

　　看完了烏龜小快的故事，是不是讓你興起養烏龜當寵物的念頭呢？下面以最常見的紅耳龜為例，列出了一些買烏龜、養烏龜時需要注意的事情，大家可要睜大眼睛仔細看囉！

 如何選到一隻好烏龜

想要挑到一隻健康的小紅耳龜，要注意牠是不是具有以下四項特徵：
1. 四肢強壯有力。
2. 龜殼沒有變白、或有像黴菌一樣的白色斑點。
3. 頭部、尾巴、四肢沒有受傷、破皮或潰爛。
4. 有充沛的食慾，餵食的時候會搶著吃。

 如何正確的飼養烏龜

1. 食物：紅耳龜幾乎什麼都吃，一般較常餵食的是龜飼料、蔬菜水果，還有小昆蟲、小蝦、和動物內臟等含豐富鈣質的食物。

2. 水缸：水缸內要放水，水深約 5 到 10 公分，要有石頭或木頭可以讓牠爬上去休息。記得要常常換水，保持水的清潔，或者裝過濾系統。天氣冷的時候可以幫小烏龜加個保溫燈、保溫棒或加溫石，這些東西都可以在水族館買到。

3. 陽光：常曬太陽可以讓烏龜更健康，但是記得千萬不要在中午太陽很大的時候，讓烏龜曝曬在陽光下！而且曬的時候也要有蔭涼的地方讓牠休息，旁邊也要有水池可以讓牠泡泡水。

4. 隔離：如果你養了兩隻以上的烏龜，又常常看見烏龜在打架，原因可能是空間太小、或者是其中一隻比較具攻擊性，這時候，把牠們分開來養會比較好喔！

現在，你是不是大概了解養紅耳龜的技巧了呢？在決定養一隻烏龜之前，要記得養寵物是需要耐性和責任感的，千萬不要半途而廢、隨意將烏龜放生，這樣不但烏龜很可憐，也會破壞自然生態的平衡喔！

寫書的人

Jill McDougall is an Australian children's writer whose first book, "Anna the Goanna," was a Children's Book Council Notable Book. Jill has written and published over eighty titles for children including short stories, picture books and novels. Jill enjoys yoga, cooking and walking her two dogs along the beach.

畫畫的人

　　王祖民，江蘇蘇州市人。現任江蘇少年兒童出版社美術編輯副編審，從事兒童讀物插圖創作工作，作品曾多次在國際國內獲獎。作品《虎丘山》曾獲聯合國科教文野間兒童讀物插圖獎。

小烏龜大麻煩系列
Turtle Trouble Series

Jill McDougall　著／王祖民　繪

附中英雙語朗讀CD／適合具基礎英文閱讀能力者(國小4-6年級)閱讀

　　烏龜小快是小女孩茱莉養的寵物，他既懶散又貪吃，還因此鬧出不少笑話，讓茱莉一家人的生活充滿歡笑跟驚奇！想知道烏龜小快發生了什麼事嗎？快看《小烏龜大麻煩系列》故事，保證讓你笑聲不斷喔！

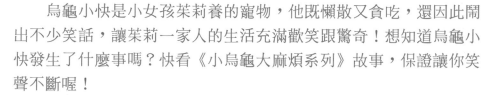

國家圖書館出版品預行編目資料

Where Is Speedy?:小快在哪裡? / Jill McDougall著;
王祖民繪;本局編輯部譯.－－初版一刷.－－臺北
市: 三民，2005
　　面；　　公分.－－(Fun心讀雙語叢書.小烏龜，大
麻煩系列⑥)
中英對照
ISBN 957–14–4325–5　　(精裝)
　　1.英國語言－讀本
523.38　　　　　　　　　　　　　94012416

網路書店位址　http://www.sanmin.com.tw

© 　Where Is Speedy?

―――小快在哪裡?

著作人　　Jill McDougall
繪　書　　王祖民
譯　書　　本局編輯部
發行人　　劉振強
著作財　　三民書局股份有限公司
產權人　　臺北市復興北路386號
發行所　　三民書局股份有限公司
　　　　　地址 / 臺北市復興北路386號
　　　　　電話 / (02)25006600
　　　　　郵撥 / 0009998–5
印刷所　　三民書局股份有限公司
門市部　　復北店 / 臺北市復興北路386號
　　　　　重南店 / 臺北市重慶南路一段61號
初版一刷　2005年8月
編　號　　S 805631
定　價　　新臺幣壹佰捌拾元整
行政院新聞局登記證局版臺業字第○二○○號

ISBN　957–14–4325–5　　(精裝)